Pull-Out Poster Book

Based on the screenplay written by
Leo Benvenuti & Steve Rudnick and Timothy Harris & Herschel Weingrod

FAMILY ENTERTAINMENT

R E A D I N G

© 1996 Warner Bros.

SCHOLASTIC INC.
New York Toronto London Auckland Sydney

ISBN 0-590-94557-2

SJSC19

12 11 10 9 8 7 6 5 4 3 2 1   6 7 8 9/9 0 1/0

Designed by Joan Ferrigno

Printed in the U.S.A.   08

First Scholastic printing, November 1996

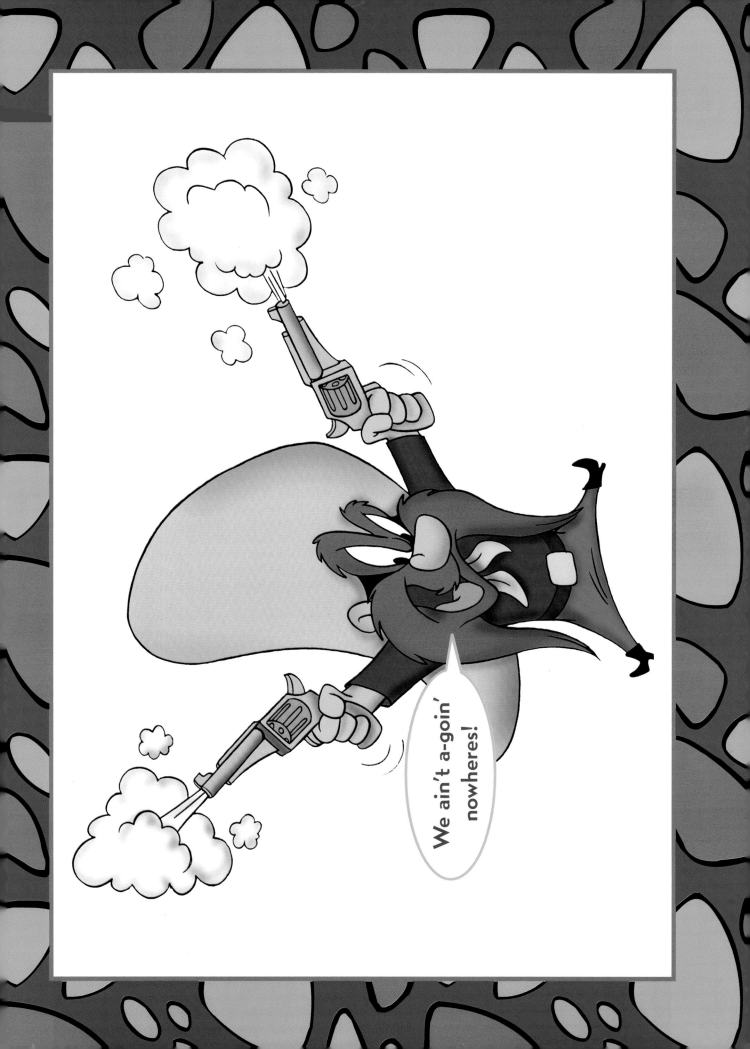